704

jE
Climo, Shirley
The cobweb Christmas

70380

P9-CFX-853

DO NOT REMOVE
CARDS FROM POCKET

Holiday Collection

APR 25 '83

HOLIDAY COLLECTION
ALLEN COUNTY PUBLIC LIBRARY

FORT WAYNE, INDIANA 46802

You may return this book to any agency, branch,
or bookmobile of the Allen County Public Library

DEMCO

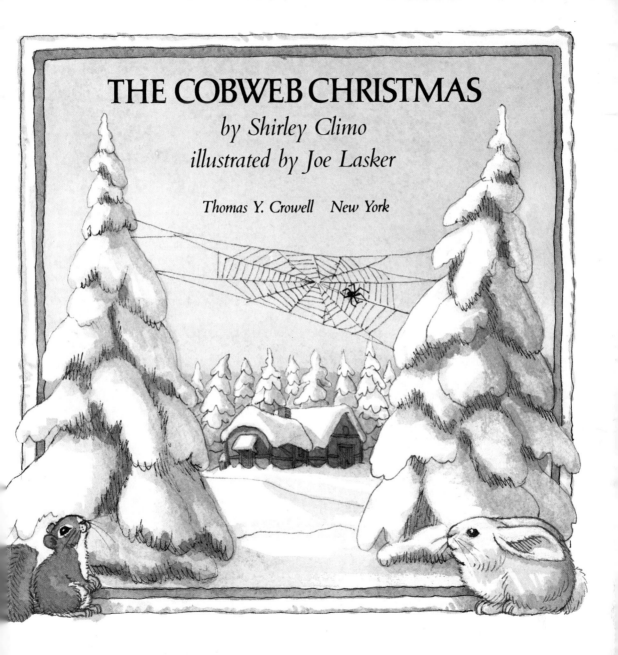

THE COBWEB CHRISTMAS

by Shirley Climo
illustrated by Joe Lasker

Thomas Y. Crowell   New York

ALLEN COUNTY PUBLIC LIBRARY
FORT WAYNE, INDIANA

ALSO BY SHIRLEY CLIMO

Piskies, Spriggans, and Other Magical Beings

The Cobweb Christmas
Text copyright © 1982 by Shirley Climo
Illustrations copyright © 1982 by Joe Lasker

All rights reserved. Printed in the United States of America.

Library of Congress Cataloging in Publication Data
Climo, Shirley.
Cobweb Christmas.
Summary: After waiting years to witness some of the
special magic that happens Christmas Eve, a kindly old
woman finally gets her wish.
[1. Christmas—Fiction]   I. Lasker, Joe, ill.
II. Title.
PZ7.C62247Co   1982   [E]   81-43879
ISBN 0-690-04215-9   AACR2
ISBN 0-690-04216-7 (lib. bdg.)

1 2 3 4 5 6 7 8 9 10
First Edition

FOR ROBERT, SUSAN, AND LISA,

WHO HELPED TO MAKE CHRISTMAS MAGIC

7038012

ONCE UPON A CHRISTMASTIME, long ago in Germany, there lived a little old woman. She was so little she had to climb upon a step stool to reach her feather bed and so old she couldn't even count all the Christmases she'd seen. The children in her village called her Tante, which means "Auntie" in German.

Tante's home was a cottage at the edge of a thick fir forest. The cottage had but one room, one door, and one window, and no upstairs to it at all. It suited the old woman, for there was room enough within its walls for her to keep a canary for singing, a cat for purring, and a dog to doze beside the fire.

Squeezed up against the cottage was a barn. The barn was a bit bigger, and in it Tante kept a donkey for riding, and a cow and a goat for milk and cheese. She had a noisy rooster as well to crow her out of bed each morning, and a speckled hen to lay an egg for her breakfast. With so many animals about, the tiny cottage wasn't tidy, but Tante didn't fuss over a few feathers, a little fur, or a spiderweb or two.

Except once a year, when the days got short and the nights grew long the old woman would nod her head and say, "Time to clean for Christmas."

Then she'd shake the quilt and wash the window and scour the soot from the kettle. She'd scrub the floor on her hands and knees and stand tiptoe on her step stool to sweep the cobwebs from the ceiling.

This Christmas was just as always.

"Wake up!" said Tante, snapping her fingers. The dog stopped dreaming and dashed off to dig for bones beneath the bushes.

"Scat!" cried Tante, flapping her apron. The cat hid under the bedclothes and the canary flew to the chimney top.

"Shoo!" scolded Tante, swishing her broom. All the spiders and each little wisp of web went flying out the door as well.

When she'd washed and wiped every crack and corner of the cottage, the old woman nodded her head and said, "Time to fetch Christmas."

Then Tante took the axe from its peg in the barn, and hung the harness with the bells upon the donkey. She scrambled onto the donkey's back, nimble as a mouse, and the two jogged and jingled into the fir forest. They circled all around, looking for a tree to fit Tante's liking.

"Too big!" said she of some, and "Crooked as a pretzel!" of others.

At last she spied a fir that grew straight, but not tall, bushy, but not wide. When the wind blew, the tree bent and bobbed a curtsey to the little old woman.

"It wants to come for Christmas," Tante told the donkey, "and so it shall."

She chopped down the tree with her axe, taking care to leave a bough or two so it might grow again. And they went home, only now the donkey trotted with the tree upon his back and the old lady skipped along beside.

The tree fit the cottage as snugly as if it had sprouted there. The top touched the rafters, and the tips of the branches brushed the window on one side and the door frame on the other. The old woman nodded her head and said, "Time to make Christmas."

Then Tante made cookies. She made gingerbread boys and girls. She baked almond cookies, cut into crescents like new moons, and cinnamon cookies, shaped like stars. When she'd sprinkled them with sugar and hung them on the tree, they looked as if they'd fallen straight from the frosty sky. Next she rubbed apples until they gleamed like glass and hung these up, too. Tante put a red ribbon on a bone for the dog and tied up a sprig of catnip for the cat. She stuck bites of cheese into pinecones for the mice and bundled bits of oats to tuck among the branches for the donkey and the cow and the goat. She strung nuts for the squirrels, wove garlands of seeds for the birds, and cracked corn into a basket for the chickens. There was something for everyone on Tante's tree, except, of course, for the spiders, for they'd been brushed away.

When she was done, the old woman nodded her head and said, "Time to share Christmas."

Tante invited all the children in the village to come and see the tree, as she did every year.

"Tante!" the children cried, "that's the most wonderful tree in the world!"

When the children had nibbled the apples and sampled the cookies, they went home to their beds to wait for Christkindel. Christkindel was the spirit who went from house to house on Christmas Eve and slipped presents into the toes of their shoes.

Then the old woman
invited the animals
to come and share Christmas.

The dog and the cat and the canary and the chickens
and some small shy wild creatures crowded into the
cottage. The donkey and the cow and the goat peered in
the window and steamed the pane with their warm breath.
To each and every visitor, Tante gave a gift.

But no one could give Tante what she wanted. All of her life the little old woman had heard stories about marvelous happenings on Christmas Eve. Cocks would crow at midnight. Bees could hum a carol. Animals might speak aloud. More than anything else, Tante wanted some Christmas magic that was not of her own making. So the old woman sat down in her rocking chair and said, "Now it's time to wait for Christmas."

She nodded and nodded and nodded her head.

Tante was tired from the cleaning and the chopping and the cooking, and she fell fast asleep. If the rooster crowed when the clock struck twelve, Tante wasn't listening. She didn't hear if the donkey whispered in the cow's ear, or see if the dog danced jigs with the cat. The old woman snored in her chair, just as always.

She never heard the rusty, squeaky voices calling at her door, "Let us in!"

Someone else heard.

Christkindel was passing the cottage on his way to take the toys to the village children. He listened. He looked and saw hundreds of spiders sitting on Tante's doorstep.

"We've never had a Christmas," said the biggest spider. "We're always swept away. Please, Christkindel, may we peek at Tante's tree?"

So Christkindel opened the cottage door a crack, just wide enough to let a little starlight in. For what harm could come from looking?

And he let the spiders in as well.

Huge spiders, tiny spiders, smooth spiders, hairy spiders, spotted spiders, striped spiders, brown and black and yellow spiders, and the palest kind of see-through spiders came

creeping, crawling, sneaking softly,
scurrying, hurrying, quickly, lightly,
zigging, zagging,
weaving, and wobbling into the old woman's cottage.

The curious spiders crept closer and closer to the tree. One, two, three skittered up the trunk. All the other spiders followed the leaders.

They ran from branch to branch, in and out, back and forth, up and down the tree. Wherever the spiders went, they left a trail behind. Threads looped from limb to limb, and webs were woven everywhere.

Now the spiders weren't curious any longer. They'd seen Christmas. They'd felt Christmas, every twig on the tree, so they scuttled away.

When Christkindel came back to latch the door he found Tante's tree tangled with sticky, stringy spiderwebs. He knew how hard the old woman had worked to clean her cottage. He understood how dismayed she'd be on Christmas morning. But he didn't blame the busy spiders. Instead he changed their cobwebs into a gift for Tante.

Christkindel touched the spokes of each web with his finger. The twisted strands turned shiny gold; the dangling threads sparkled like silver. Now the old woman's Christmas tree was truly the most wonderful in the world.

The rooster woke Tante in the morning.

"What's this?" cried Tante. She rubbed her eyes and blinked at the glittering tree. "Something marvelous has happened!"

Tante was puzzled, as well as pleased. So she climbed on her stool, the better to see how such magic was spun. At the tip top of the tree, one teeny, tiny spider, unnoticed by Christkindel, was finishing its web.

"Now I know why this Christmas is not like any other," said Tante.

The little old woman knew, too, that such miracles come but once. So, each Christmastime thereafter, she did not clean so carefully, but left a few webs in the rafters, so that the spiders might share Christmas. And every year, after she'd hung the cookies and the apples and the garlands on her tree, the little old woman would nod her head and say, "Time for Christmas magic."

Then Tante would weave tinsel among the branches, until the tree sparkled with strings of gold and silver. Just as her tree did on the Cobweb Christmas.

Just as Christmas trees do today.